# SEVEN TALES FROM KING ARTHUR'S COURT

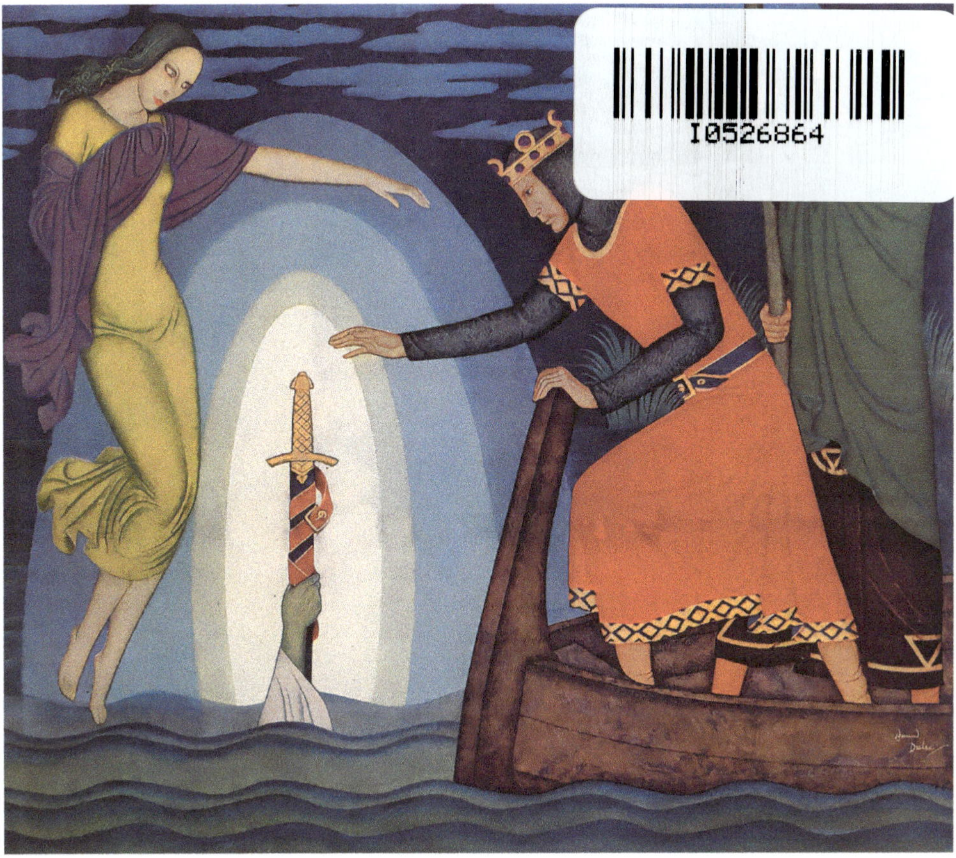

PAINTINGS BY EDMUND DULAC
TEXT BY JOHN ERSKINE
EDITED BY ALBERT SELIGMAN

FIRST PRINTING, March 2023.
Harry Markos, Director.

*Paperback:* ISBN 978-1-915860-09-5
*eBook:* ISBN 978-1-915860-10-1


*Book design by: Ian Sharman*




www.markosia.com

First Edition

# INTRODUCTION

 *he American Weekly* magazine was a Sunday supplement published by the Hearst Corporation from 1896 until 1966. They claimed a circulation of over 50 million readers and it was carried by at least seventeen of the Hearst newspapers. Each edition was usually between 12 and 24 pages and was printed on very cheap and fragile newsprint, so not many intact copies survive today. Like most Sunday supplements of the time, it was filled with sensationalism and illustrations of scantily clad females, and some fiction articles as well. However, the front cover art was really notable. In addition to Edmund Dulac, the front cover artists were some of the most famous of the times, including Howard Chandler Christy (the Christy Girls), James Montgomery Flagg, Erté, Leon Bakst, Virgil Finlay (also known for his pulp magazine covers), Henry Clive, Alberto Vargas, Nell Brinkley (the Queen of the Comics), Zoe Mozert and many others.

Public domain image provided by Grapefruit Moon Gallery
(Henry Clive Hearst Corporation)

In 1940 *The American Weekly* published a series of "Seven Tales from King Arthur's Court" illustrated by Edmund Dulac with the text written by John Erskine. We were very fortunate to find copies of the Dulac series in wonderful condition in the collection of the San Francisco Academy of Comic Art. The curator, Bill Blackbeard, allowed us to photograph the covers using a high-quality film camera. These images have been digitized and have been used in the preparation of this book.

## Edmund Dulac

Much has been written about Edmund Dulac since his death in 1953 from his third heart attack. He was born in Toulouse France in 1882 and was educated as a lawyer, although he rebelled and later studied art at the Ecole des Beaux Arts. He is best known for his book illustrations and designs of postage stamps and banknotes.

London, July 1, 1914, New York Public Library, PD-US

Dulac emigrated to England from France in 1904 and was in London at exactly the right time for the invention of color separation photographic reproduction. Prior to color separation process printers relied on wood blocks or expensive and complicated chromo-lithography to include color illustrations in their books. Most illustrators (Arthur Rackham and Heath Robinson for example) used line drawings to hold the difference in the color changes. Dulac was a watercolorist and this new technique allowed him to paint the colors just as he normally would for a painting, without bold lines defining his subjects. He received numerous commissions for the new gift books with full color tipped-in plates mounted on heavy art paper.

He began an arrangement with both Leicester Galleries and Hodder & Stoughton, the book publishers, to paint watercolors for their illustrated gift book editions which would be sold in the gallery exhibit once a year. He produced 50 oriental style drawings for *The Arabian Nights* in 1907, 40 drawings for an edition of *The Tempest* in 1908, 20 watercolors, again in his now signature orientalism style, for *The Rubaiyat of Omar Khayyam* in 1909. Subsequent editions were *The Sleeping Beauty and Other Fairy Tales* in 1910, *Stories from Hans Christian Andersen* in 1911, and 28 watercolors with dozens of line illustrations for *The Bells and Other Poems* by Edgar Allan Poe in 1912. After the first World War he illustrated only three more gift books, the last being one of his finest in a Persian miniature style, using gold and silver metallic inks. *The Kingdom of the Pearl* by Leonard Rosenthal was released in 1920 with a beautiful soft cover French edition in Paris, and two English language editions in London and New York. In spite of the book's critical acclaim, it was remaindered, although it is greatly sought after today.

In 1923, *"Edmund Dulac, the Distinguished English Artist,"* as he was billed on the covers, was contracted by the Hearst organization to paint watercolors for *The American Weekly* Sunday magazine. The contract lasted 30 years and Dulac painted 107 watercolors for thirteen different series until his last *Tales from the Arabian Nights* in 1951. "Seven Tales from King Arthur's Court" was published in 1940, just as World War II was intensifying for the British. 'Arthur will return at the hour of Britain's greatest need' the legend of Camelot says, and may have been the motivation to release this series at this time.

# John Erskine

Photograph shows John Erskine with daughter, Anna Erskine Crouse, wife,
Pauline Ives Erskine, and son, Graham Erskine. Circa 1930 Library of Congress

The text accompanying these illustrations was written by John Erskine, who was an author, pianist and composer. He was born in New York City in 1879 and raised in Weehawken, New Jersey. He was an English professor at Amherst College from 1903 to 1909 and taught at Columbia University from 1909 to 1937. He was also the first president of Juilliard School of Music from 1928 to 1937 and the director of the New York Metropolitan Opera Association. He published over 100 books, novels and essays, including *The Moral Obligation to be Intelligent* in 1915 and *The Private Life of Helen of Troy* in 1925, which was made into a film in 1927. In 1928 he published *The Delight of Great Books* which included a chapter on Sir Thomas Malory's *Le Morte d'Arthur*, reproduced here. He was responsible for the Great Books academic movement that was part of the core curriculum at Columbia University. It later inspired *The Great Books of the Western World* published by the Encyclopedia Britannica; a mammoth 60 volume set of literature from works of the ancient Greeks to Ernest Hemmingway. He died in New York in 1951 at age 71.

Following each text is a short **Who Was?** paragraph explaining the various characters of each Tale. We don't know exactly who wrote these for the Hearst Corporation, but suspect it is Watson Crewes, Jr. who was a contributing writer.

*"Since Malory's time many writers have used these legends and retold them in their own language. The English authors Tennyson, Swinburne, Matthew Arnold and William Morris have rendered several of the old stories in verse. And noteworthy too, are Wagner's magnificent music dramas Parsifal, which recounts the legend of the Holy Grail and Tristan and Isolda, perhaps the most famous love story of all times. Mr. John Erskine is now added to this company of distinguished interpreters, who retells them delightfully for readers of The American Weekly".*

Attributed to Watson Crewes, Jr., *The American Weekly*, February 4, 1940

## Acknowledgments

I would like to thank Taylan Coppola for her help with transcribing and editing. Special thanks to Ann Hughey for her contributions and constant encouragement with *The American Weekly* archive collection. Many thanks to Bud Plant and Jim Vadeboncoeur, America's consummate illustrated book collectors, for their many additions to my book collections over the years and advice on this project.

Bill Blackbeard's complete collection of the American Weekly covers now reside at The Billy Ireland Cartoon Library & Museum at Ohio State University and I thank their staff for assistance in my research.

Grapefruit Moon Gallery let me reproduce some of their photos of *The American Weekly* covers from their fabulous website.

Peter Harrington Company of London also provided artwork, many thanks.

I am grateful to Elizabeth Beeton for designing the front cover, and Cristina and Cassandra of Nubes for the back cover.

Front Cover, *Le Mort d' Arthur*, Sir Thomas Malory, published by Dent 1902 with Aubrey Beardsley illustrations, Library of Congress, PD-US

# TABLE OF CONTENTS

Introduction

*The Delight of Great Books* by John Erskine

## *Seven Tales from King Arthur's Court*

First Tale - *The Tale of Arthur's Sword "Excalibur"*

Second Tale - *The Tale of Sir Tristram and the Love Potent*

Third Tale - *The Tale of the Enchantress and the Magic Scabbard*

Fourth Tale - *The Tale of Sir Galahad and his Quest for the Sangreal*

Fifth Tale - *The Tale of Lancelot and the Four Queens*

Sixth Tale - *The Tale of Merlin and One of the Ladies of the Lake*

Seventh Tale - *The Tale of How Sir Lancelot Slew Sir Agravaine*

Further Reading

Editors' Notes

*The Delight of Great Books*
Eveleigh Nash & Greyson Limited
London, 1928

## MALORY'S LE MORTE D'ARTHUR

When William Caxton, the great English printer, set the type for Sir Thomas Malory's *Morte d'Arthur,* he provided the famous book with a preface which is still the most illuminating introduction to it. At the end of the fifteenth century printing was still so unusual an art and the printer felt his office so important, that any book that he took the pains to publish would, in his opinion, deserve a special comment. Caxton says that he has put out various histories, "as well of contemplation as of other historical and worldly acts of great conquers and princes." His reason for bringing out now this collection of stories about King Arthur is that many English gentlemen asked him if it was not the time to print the history of the Holy Grail, and the exploits of the chief of the three Christian worthies. Caxton, in a large parenthesis, explains to the reader that of the famous nine worthies of history, three were pagans, three were Jews and three were Christians. The pagans were Hector of Troy, Alexander the Great and Julius Caesar. The three Jews were Joshua, David and Judas Maccabaeus. The three Christians were King Arthur, Charlemagne and Godfrey of Bouillon, and the greatest of these all was King Arthur.

*The Birth, Life, and Acts of King Arthur, of His Noble Knights of the Round Table, Their Marvellous Enquests and Adventures, the Achieving of the San Greal and in the End Le Morte d'Arthur, with the Dolorous Death and Departing Out of This World of Them All*, two volumes. First Beardsley edition of Malory's Arthurian epic, vellucent binding by Cedric Chivers, hand-painted after Beardsley's own artwork within. London: J. M. Dent, 1893. Public domain scan provided by Peter Harrington Co. London

Caxton says that he raised some doubts as to whether King Arthur had ever existed. Throughout the preface we feel that the greatest printer has a keen critical sense, and much humor. The ease with which he is convinced by his friends suggests charm of character rather than credulity. He says his friends answered that it would be folly and blindness to doubt that King Arthur had lived, because in the first place anyone can see where he is buried in the Monastery of Glastonbury. And also there are books which mention him, and in Westminster Abbey there is a print of a seal which is said to be his; and at the castle of Dover there is a skull which is said to be Gawaine's; and at Winchester a table which is said to be the famous Round Table; and in another place Lancelot's sword, and other similar evidence.

King Arthur's Round Table at Winchester Castle - Winchester, Hampshire, England
August Swerdferger PD-US

"All these things considered," concludes Caxton, "there can no man reasonably say but there was a king of this land named Arthur." Having allowed himself to be convinced, he accepted the manuscript of a certain Sir Thomas Malory, an elaborate account of King Arthur and of his chief knights, translated and paraphrased and "reduced into English". Who Sir Thomas Malory was we do not know. Excellent guesses have been made by competent scholars, but he still is in the comfortable position of having his book speak for him.

Caxton says the book, beginning with the birth of Arthur and ending with his death, includes much other matter, as indeed it does. It treats, he says, of noble acts, feats of arms, of chivalry, prowess, hardiness, humanity, love, courtesy, and very gentleness, with many wonderful histories and adventures. It is divided into twenty-one books, each one devoted to some central character or theme, a list of which he gives, but through all of them the same characters come and go- Arthur and Guinevere, Lancelot, Merlin, Tristram, Iseult, Sir Bors, Sir Gawaine, and the others.

Like the good printer he was, Caxton felt that his art must justify itself in the improvement of mankind. He says, therefore, that he has printed the stories to the intent that noble men may see and learn the noble acts of chivalry, the gentle and virtuous deeds that some knights used in those days, by which they came to honor; and how they that were vicious were punished and oft put to shame and rebuke. Oft, but not always. The fact is that Sir Thomas Malory had gathered so much and so miscellaneous a group of stories around the central figure of Arthur that no one simple philosophy could explain all of them, and as Caxton goes on to describe in some detail the variety of plot and character, one sees the prospect of wide disagreement as to what is moral in the book and what isn't. "Herein may be seen noble chivalry, courtesy, humanity, friendliness, hardiness, love, friendship, cowardness, hate, virtue and sin." But Caxton solves all the critical problems by one general bit of good advice- the best solution of all questions of censorship in art. "Do after the good and leave the evil, and it shall bring you to good fame and renown." He also gives us a hint that all the events in this marvelous volume may not be strictly historical- there are too many dragons and too many magicians in it. It will be pleasant to read it, he says, but "for to give faith and believe that all is true that is contained herein, ye be at your liberty"

What we have here, then, is first of all a collection of great stories. The *Morte d'Arthur* is one of those priceless volumes in which, through the genius of one man, or what seems a happy accident, the best stories which have delighted the world for hundreds of years are at last, and just before it would be too late, gathered up and made available for prosperity. If Malory had not brought together these Arthurian tales, it might have been difficult for Spenser to discover them: we might have had no *Faerie Queen*, and in the nineteenth century we might not have had Tennyson's *Idylls*. When we begin to read Malory, the initial pleasure for most of us is in recognizing the characters and legends which succeeding writers took from him.

*Faerie Queene* by Edmund Spenser, a poem in six books
George Allen publisher, 1897, Walter Crane illustrator

But *Morte d'Arthur* is far more than a source book- it is itself a great story, and holds its high place in literature by its own peculiar merits. We miss some of its quality so long as we try to find in it merely a resemblance here and there to Spenser, or to Tennyson, or to some other poet who has retold the legend of Arthur. If we judge Malory directly from his book, without these oblique comparisons, we shall probably notice that the writers he resembles most are those who have not borrowed from him. He may make us think, now and then, of Chaucer, and of the poet who wrote *Beowulf*- both of them his predecessors, of old English and Scottish ballads, of Doctor Johnson, even to take an example from our times, of Rudyard Kipling. That is, these stories about Arthur are told not as they were, we suspect, in the French originals, but with modifications dictated by a very English temperament- by a character which liked clear cut events, down right talk and positive conduct, and which found satisfaction in a dramatic fight. For the mysticism of the grail legend, for the romance of Lancelot's love or Tristram's, we must go elsewhere. It is a waste of time to read much of either into this book. But we find here in perfection that child-like zest in events for their own sake which is present in folk tales, and in fairy tales, and in all the myths which have haunted the race's memory. Man likes his stories to be frankly a yarn. "Once upon a time" is a fair beginning we think, and from that point on we want something to happen. Malory shared this average taste, and he had also that preference which we have called English, for those happenings which are vigorous, physical, even brutal. In the *Morte d'Arthur* the knights are said to be gentle, but they hit hard, and they habitually get hurt, and they are familiar with battle, murder and sudden death.

"How Morgan Le Fay gave a Shield to Sir Tristram",
*The Birth, Life, and Acts of King Arthur, of His Noble Knights of the Round Table,*
Dent,1893, Aubrey Beardsley illustrator PD-US

We are amazed to notice what terrific scenes are reported without comment and without emotion. Sir Archade accused Sir Palamides of treason- to take one example- and of course Sir Palamides challenges him to mortal combat. They were urged not to fight until after dinner, so they dined first. Then they got on their horses, fully armed, and Lancelot and the Queen and others sat down to watch, as though it might be a tennis match. It may have been late in the afternoon before they began, but the fight was disappointingly short. The first time the horses ran at each other, Palamides lifted Archade on his spear over the horse's tail. Then he dismounted and drew his sword, but Archade couldn't get up, so he cut his head off. Then, we are told, they all went in for supper.

*The Arming and Departure of the Knights*, one of the Holy Grail-themed 19th-century tapestries by Edward Burne-Jones, William Morris, and John Henry Dearle. This version woven by Morris & Co. for Lawrence Hodson of Compton Hall 1895-96. Wool and silk on cotton warp. Birmingham Museum and Art Gallery.PD-US

The superficial impression of a first reading is that in the zest for incident Malory has little discrimination; one event is a good as another, and there is no effect of relief or emphasis. It was as though he were imitating the flatness of an old tapestry. Perhaps he was. Perhaps his readers once felt in the stories an emphasis to which we are now unresponsive. One suspects something of this sort in the story of Tor, the son of King Pellinore. A poor man came to court one day, bringing with him a tall youth of eighteen, riding on a lean mare. It was the time of Arthur's marriage, and the rumor was that the happy monarch would grant any boon asked of him- unless it was unreasonable. So, this poor man, a cowherd, asked him to make the tall youth a knight. I have thirteen sons, he said, and the others are all willing to work at anything I tell them, but this one is quite useless; he spends his time shooting and casting spears and watching gentlemen fight, and he wants to be a knight himself. The King, impressed with the boy's size, asked to see the other twelve, but they all looked like the poor man. So, the King, in his good nature, knighted Tor, and then asked Merlin whether the new addition to the order would be a success. Merlin replied that the boy ought to be, since his father was not the cowherd but King Pellinore. The cowherd said he rather thought not, but when his wife was brought, she admitted the fact. I knew nothing about this, said the cowherd, but it may well be, for he doesn't resemble me in the slightest. The only person offended seems to have been the boy. Dishonor not my mother, he said to Merlin- a little late as his mother had just confessed. But Merlin explained that the news was more for his honor than his hurt, since his father was a good man and a king. When Pellinore happened to arrive in court the next day, Arthur told him that they had found a son of his, and Pellinore was greatly pleased.

Perhaps the early readers of Malory could understand why this incident should give so much pleasure all around. For us, the apparent disregard for the moral situation and of the psychology of the characters produces an effect of quaintness, if not of comedy. This particular incident serves as a good illustration because throughout the book we come on stories of heroes whose birth is accounted for irregularly or mysteriously. A mystery surrounds the birth of Arthur, and magic is involved in the birth of Galahad. Many of the knights, if their origin is shadowed by no mystery, are at least descended from an ancestry that needs explaining. The medieval reader had theories about fortunate birth which we do not feel, and in this aspect of Malory's book we encounter an outworn point of view, and are reminded that the book is old. But even in such places an effect survives for us; an effect for human drama, or of light on human motives, or, as in the case of Tor, an incidental effect of quiet comedy. The modern reader will be wise if she/he worries little about the original intent of such passages, and accepts with gratitude the charming effect they now make on her/him.

"The Enchanter Merlin" from *The Story of King Arthur and his Knights*,
1903 George Newnes, Limited- Howard Pyle illustrator PD-US

When anyone writes a story, she/he finds her/himself solving the plot in one of two ways, according to temperament. Either the incidents will be resolved by other incidents, or else they will come to an end, as experience often does in life, without any special climax, but with a byproduct of illumination and understanding. In the first kind of story, it is our will which is aroused. We feel for the hero who is in danger, or is about to be very happy, and we unconsciously desire to realize the escape or happiness proposed by the plot. Primitive stories are largely of this kind, and the vast majority of the legends in *Morte d'Arthur* are told in this manner, even though in the older versions from which Malory drew them, they have rather the effect of illumination.

This other kind of story, which does not appeal to the will power, stimulates in us an understanding of life. It gives us insight into people, and at last into ourselves. Its end is not action, but clarification. In Malory there are a few episodes of this kind, but for the most part, the clarifying effect is illustrated incidentally by occasional passages indicating that Malory had the gift, but implying that he preferred the other sort of plot.

This differentiation between the two types of stories perhaps clears up for us a vague feeling we get from the book- a feeling which I have just tried to describe by saying that Malory is essentially English. He belongs to the race which holds that conduct is three-fourths, or a little more, of life. And we get the impression that like Doctor Johnson he would say that the rules of human conduct are well understood by the normally intelligent, and nothing remains but to act them out. Malory's world has no subtleties in it. Its morality is not always ours, and in some places, we wonder just what its standards were, but in no place do we suspect any very fine distinctions, nor any problem which could not be settled by the simplest sort of character. Later English poets, using the same material, have made it subtle once more as it was in several of the old versions which Malory "reduced into English". The point is worth laboring somewhat, for most readers coming on Malory after having read Tennyson (*Idylls of the King*) instinctively try to find in the old book what they have loved in the modern poet. It is helpful, perhaps, to notice at once how often the stories are simply records of action, ending happily or disastrously, without comment and without even a suggested philosophy. Here and there we also come on the other kind of narrative, and observe the sudden clarification of character which lights up the bare sweep of the epic.

Portrait of Tennyson, Paul Rajon, artist, NY 1888
Library of Congress copy PD-US

A typical incident is the fight between King Arthur and the giant. The giant was a very bad man and had conquered fifteen kings, whose beards he had shaved off and used in embroidering his coat. Also- we are not sure this is the greater crime- the giant is a cannibal. Arthur decides to rid the land of such a monster, and finds him on the crest of the hill, where he sat at supper gnawing a human limb, waited on by three fair captive ladies, who were roasting before the fire, under compulsion, of course, twelve young children, new born, like young birds. Malory does not mind heaping up the gruesome details. King Arthur challenges the giant, calling him a glutton, which he certainly was. The glutton started up, and with a great club knocked the king's crown off. Thereupon King Arthur, reaching up as far as he could, wounded this immense creature, and the giant in desperation threw away the club, caught the king in his arms, and began crushing his ribs. In this mortal wrestling the two began to roll down the hill; says Malory, "they went weltering and wallowing" till they came to the edge of the sea at the bottom of the mountain. And every time Arthur came on top in these revolutions, he managed to stab the giant with his dagger. When they reached level ground they ceased to roll, and Arthur got up and saw that his enemy was dead.

"This was the fiercest giant I ever met with," said Arthur, "except one on the Mount of Araby which I overcame, but this was greater and fiercer." As Malory tells the incident we have the proper melodramatic concern for the king. When he survives the fight, we are satisfied, and we take a final pleasure from the nonchalant tone with which he compares giants like a connoisseur. This is Malory's way of unfolding incidents with broad strokes, and with the solution which our own wills prompt.

"Faire virgin to redeem her deare,
Brings Arthur to the fight:
Who slays the Gyanunt, wounds the beast,
And strips Duessa guight"
*Faerie Queene* by Edmund Spenser, a poem in six books
George Allen publisher, 1897, Walter Crane illustrator  PD-US

One or two other stories might serve chiefly for contrast. When Meliagrance (Maleagant) accused the queen of treason and Lancelot came to rescue her, the fight is told in unusual detail, and there is more in it of psychology and perhaps of incidental illumination. Meliagrance, according to Malory, was a desperate traitor, and knowing that Lancelot would oppose him on the fatal day, he set a trap for the great knight, and had him imprisoned in a dungeon from which he was not to get out until after the queen's cause was lost and she was burned at the stake. In the castle in which the dungeon was, a fair lady lost her heart to Lancelot, and visited him each day, asking him for his love. If he would love her, she said, she would release him in time for him to rescue the queen. Lancelot remained loyal to Guinevere, saying, though it was not his choice to be free, it was his duty to be true. On the very morning of the judicial combat the lady repented, and told Lancelot that if he would at least give her one kiss, that she would release him. Lancelot says that by all the codes of honor with which he is familiar, one kiss does not count, so he will buy his freedom on those terms. He arrives on the field at the last moment, and naturally he comes with murder in his heart. At the first encounter with Meliagrance it is quite obvious that Lancelot will win. Meliagrance, struck down, cries out for mercy, confessing that he was in the wrong. Lancelot was greatly disappointed at this result, for he could not decline to yield the mercy asked for, yet he was determined to kill Meliagrance. And as he stood there perplexed, he noticed that the queen nodded to him, as though she would say, "Kill him." So, Lancelot asked Meliagrance to get up and fight again. Meliagrance declined. Lancelot then offered him a generous handicap; he would unarm his head, the left quarter of his body and let his left hand be tied behind his back and then fight him. The offer seemed so good that Meliagrance accepted the offer, jumped to his feet and began the battle again on those terms. When he came on with his sword raised, Lancelot showed his bare head and left side defenseless, but as Maliagrance brought the sword down on him, he dodged the blow lightly and cut the rascal's head in two. Malory says there was nothing more to do but to bury him.

"I am Sir Lancelot du Lake, King Ban's son of Benwick, and knight of the Round Table."
*The Boy's King Arthur,*1922- N. C. Wyeth illustrator

An incident in another key belongs to the story of Tristram and Iseult, and Kehydius, the brother of that other Iseult whom Tristram had married in Brittany. Tristram had married this Iseult out of gratitude, but he did not love her, and she was his wife only in name. Kehydius followed Tristram back to Cornwall, and when he saw the great Iseult, he fell in love with her, to the annoyance of Tristram. He wrote letters to her, secretly, and ballads, "of the most goodliest that were used in those days." Fair Iseult was not in love with him, but she was so sorry for his plight that unwisely she wrote him a letter "to comfort him withal." And one day when King Mark was playing chess in the garden under a window, Sir Tristram was in a room upstairs asking Iseult what the letters meant- unluckily that had come to his notice. Kehydius was there also, and though the interview started with rational explanations, it ended in an attempt by Tristram to kill his rival, who saved himself by jumping out of the window, over the head of the king as he sat playing chess. When the king saw someone come hurling over his head he said, "Fellow, what art thou and what is the cause thou leapest out at that window?" "My lord the king," said Kehydius, "it fortuned me that I was asleep in the window above your head, and as I slept, I slumbered, and so I fell down." And thus Sir Kehydius excused him. Here the point of the story seems to have been the proud sagacity of Sir Kehydius.

"How Sir Tristram Drank of the Love Drink", *The Birth, Life, and Acts of King Arthur, of His Noble Knights of the Round Table,* Dent 1893, Aubrey Beardsley illustrator

Here and there in the whole book one comes upon phrases of the clarifying sort which bring up a picture of human nature easily recognizable as true to experience today. The modern reader prizes these occasional glimpses perhaps more than the long account of battles and tournaments, exciting though these latter often are. We like, for example, the description of the coming of Elaine to Arthur's court, and her encounter with Guinevere. This is the first Elaine, the mother of Galahad. Malory says that she went to the court in pursuit of her lover, who hated her for having ensnared him with magic. Guinevere, of course, knows who she is. The two women, Malory says, smiled at each other, "but nothing with hearts." We like the very human way in which Lancelot's conscience begins to trouble him for his sins. He begins to repent only when he becomes unlucky. He got into a very dangerous place and suddenly discovered himself deprived of horse and arms. When he saw that these were missing, says Malory, he knew that God must be displeased at him.

"Guinevere and Sir Bors", *The Book of Romance*,
Andrew Lang,1902, H.J. Ford illustrator PD-US

The one long passage in which insight into human nature takes the place of mere incident is in the closing account of Lancelot and Guinevere. Here Malory is affected by the example of his French sources. He attends rather more to the psychology of his characters than is usual with him. Perhaps also the very moving story which he is telling arouses even his somewhat practical temperament to the sense of subtle tragedy. He reports that after Arthur died, Lancelot called his men together and said that his fighting was over, but he would ride by himself and seek his lady, Queen Guinevere. So he rode into Arthur's realm unattended, though Sir Bors warned him of danger. No man nor child should be with him when he met the queen. After a search of a week or more he came to a nunnery, and Queen Guinevere, as she walked in the cloister, recognized him. She fainted at the sight, and explained to the ladies and gentlemen who came to her aid that the knight yonder had brought this sudden weakness on her. Then with Sir Lancelot standing before her she said, "Through this man and me hath all this war been wrought, and the death of the most noblest knight in the world, and through our love was my most noble lord slain." Thereafter, she goes on to say, she is resolved to save her soul in prayer and meditation, hoping even after a life of sin to have a sight of the blessed face of God. All that she asked of Sir Lancelot was to promise that he would nevermore come into her presence.

"Lancelot bears off Guinevere", frontispiece,
*The Book of Romance* by Andrew Lang, H.J. Ford, illustrator 1902 PD-US

So far, we might think that Guinevere has simply repented of her sins, and wishes to dismiss Lancelot, but the drama begins in her next words. She urges him for all the love that ever was between them to go back to his own kingdom and protect it from war and harm, and especially, she tells him, to find a wife there and live with her in joy and bliss. If he so desires, he might pray for the queen, that God might help her to repent. Out of all this speech Lancelot, of course, sizes on one stinging remark. "Do you really mean," he asks, "that you want me to go back to my country and there marry somebody? You know perfectly I'll never do that. On the contrary, if you have decided to undertake this religious life, I will do so too, and my prayers will be especially for you." Guinevere replies with some of the old coquetry, "If thou will do so, hold thy promise, but I may never believe but that thou wilt turn to the world again." Lancelot is somewhat exasperated at this in the presence of the nuns, but with self-control he bids her talk as she likes, since she knows in her heart that he loved her and her alone. He calls God to witness that in her he has had his earthly joy, and if she had been so disposed, he would have taken her into his own realm to be his queen. Since her will is otherwise, he will be a hermit. Therefore, he will leave her, but he asks for just one kiss before he goes. The queen declines, but it is clear enough that she loves him, and when he is gone, she falls into a faint. Later he hears the sad news that she is dying, and starts with several brother monks to her death bed, but we are told that her last breath was a prayer that she might never have power to see Lancelot again with her earthy eyes. Evidently, she did not trust her own good resolutions if she should meet him again.

Here Malory treats the characters in that human way which we like to call modern, but which is universal and, so far as art is concerned, immortal. If I seem to say he does this rarely, I mean only that his genius was for that other kind of narrative in which action is the chief interest. Aristotle said long ago, and we have no reason to differ with him now, that a play or a story can be good, even without character portrayal, if it has a plot; but without plot, there can be no good story, not even though the characters are closely studied. Malory has the genius for incidents, a rarer genius perhaps than the ability to merely make a plot. He makes us feel the vitality of events, as though life were enormously interesting to us, and that anything that happened were[*sic*] worth noticing. What he could do in this other realm of human nature he shows in the parting of Lancelot and Guinevere.

The *Morte d'Arthur* is full of marvelous episodes, magic, necromancy, special revelations from heaven. This material Malory inherits from his sources, but we suspect that he had not the temperament to make much of it. Merlin appears in several places, but not in an important role. The mystic sage to whom Tennyson restored a certain significance is in Malory not much more important than Dame Brisen of the other necromances. Malory's inability to handle this sort of material shows itself chiefly, of course, in his account of Galahad. He gives the episode of Galahad's birth with full attention to the supernatural elements in it, but with no great zest for what he is saying. When Elaine goes to the court and with Dame Brisen's aid lures Lancelot once more, and when Guinevere finds out this involuntary faithlessness of her lover and quarrels with Elaine, we feel that Malory is much more interested himself- certainly he tells the episode with greater vividness for us. His best use of supernatural material was probably in the account of the coming and the passing of Arthur, which had never been told in English. The wonderful story of King Uther Pendragon shows Merlin in his power and portrays the solid life of the old warfare and the old romance with a certain abandon and vigor not often matched in literature. At the other end of the book the character of Arthur in his old age seems to us perhaps inglorious if we go back to it from Tennyson. But it is consistent, and at the very end superb. According to Malory, Arthur did not greatly love Guinevere; at least not at the close of his life. Before he had married her, Merlin had warned him in vain that she would love Lancelot instead. When the Round Table was broken up by Lancelot's treachery it was for the loss of his friend rather than the loss of his queen that Arthur felt the deepest regret, and he condemned Guinevere to be burned at the stake. Lancelot rescued Guinevere, of course. In the fight round the place of execution Lancelot killed some of his own friends, especially the brothers of Sir Gawaine. They were in the crowd unarmed, and in the confusion, he did not notice whom he was striking. It is this accidental killing of some men who had been his friends which brings on the war with King Arthur. The loss of Guinevere would hardly have been enough to make trouble, for we have reason to think the king knew of her deception long before, and had decided to put up with it. In one of the last chapters we are told that Lancelot and King Arthur talked it over. Arthur and Gawaine were besieging him in his castle. The king invited Lancelot to come out and fight him, man to man, but Lancelot declined to raise his hand personally against the king. "Fie upon thy fair language," said the king, "for I am thy mortal foe. Thou hast slain my good knights." He adds also as a second item that Lancelot has carried off the queen. Lancelot immediately defends himself as to the murder of the knights, admitting his fault and repentance. As for Queen Guinevere, his answer is a curious one, that there is no knight in the world, leaving the king aside for the moment, who would dare make good that charge against him in judicial combat. He goes on to better argument when he reminds the king of the number of times Arthur had been ready to burn Guinevere at the stake- a curious record on the part of a devoted husband. Lancelot admits that he has loved the queen more than that. The rest of the conversation degenerates into recrimination, and challenge, and insult, in the way of the old battle stories, but enough has been quoted to show where the emphasis lay in the mind of King Arthur. He was interested in his knights and his Round Table, and Queen Guinevere was not a matter of great concern.

"Lancelot Brings Guinevere to Arthur",
from Andrew Lang's *The Book of Romance*, 1902 by H.J. Ford PD-US

At the end of the story Arthur is wounded in battle, and Sir Lucan and Sir Benivere carry him from the field. Tennyson has taken this splendid episode as the basis for his *Passing of Arthur*, but not even his glorious poem is finer than Malory's account. For once incident and mysticism are blended, and we listen to the convincing story of Sir Bedivere ordered to throw Excalibur away in the sea, and hesitating to lose such a priceless weapon. We see by the water side the little barge with many fair ladies in it, and among them a queen, and we watch the knight and the lady lifting the dying Arthur into the barge. Sir Bevidere's cry has lost no truth, no poignancy with the centuries: "Ah, my lord Arthur, what shall become of me, now ye go from me and leave me here alone among mine enemies?" "Comfort thyself," said the king, "and do as well as thou mayest, for in me is no trust for to trust in; for I will into the vale of Avilion to heal me of my grievous wound: and if thou hear nevermore of me, pray for my soul."

Then the King…ran towards Sir Mordred, crying, "Traitor, now is thy death day come."
- *The Boy's King Arthur* 1922 N. C. Wyeth illustrator

Malory tells the story of Lancelot and Arthur at full length. He gives the same elaborate attention to the adventures of Tristram and Iseult. The part of this famous story which interests the modern reader most is the beginning, a section of Tristram's life usually omitted from later versions, but essential to the understanding of the quarrel between King Mark and the young hero. Here Malory is following old sources rather closely. King Mark was troubled by the tyranny of the Irish monarch who levied a heavy tax on the Cornish realm. Tristram grew up to be such a powerful champion that he undertook to fight out the question of the tax in a duel with Sir Marhaus. He wounded Marhaus so severely that, though the Irish warrior managed to get home, he died with a piece of Tristram's' sword in his brain.

"How la Beale Isoud nursed Sir Tristram"
*The Birth, Life, and Acts of King Arthur, of His Noble Knights of the Round Table,* Dent 1893,
Aubrey Beardsley illustrator

Tristram himself was wounded by the poison arms of Sir Marhaus, and sooner or later realized that if ever he was to be cured, he must go to the people who invented the poison. He therefore went in disguise to the land of his enemies and was there cured by the young Iseult and her mother, relatives of the champion he had murdered. Before he left for Cornwall, however, they discovered that the fragment of steel which they had found in Marhaus's skull fitted the broken place in Tristram's sword, and if certain impulses of hospitality had not intervened, together with an incipient love for Tristram on the part of Iseult, he never would have got away. When he left, therefore, he understood that his life would not be worth much if ever he set foot in Ireland again.

On his return King Mark was grateful to him, but later on the two men, uncle and nephew, fell in love with the same woman, and the lady preferred Tristram. King Mark's jealousy prompted him to murderous intrigue. When an official marriage was arranged between him and Iseult, he insisted that Tristram, unless he wished to confess himself a coward, should go to Ireland and bring Iseult to him. Tristram undertook the journey realizing that his uncle expected something evil to happen to him. This background of rivalry and hate explains somewhat the ease with which Tristram appropriates his uncle's bride, and in the incidental account of it Malory supplies us once more with brilliant insight into human nature. The story of Balin and Balan, the story of Gareth and Lynett, and other stories familiar in Tennyson, are also recounted at length. What Malory stands for, however, in English literature is chiefly his account of Arthur and Guinevere, of Lancelot and Galahad, of Tristram and Iseult. And the peculiarity of the account is the dramatic vigor of the incidents, as against the psychological interpretation which is the charm of most other versions.

John Erskine

"King Mark slew the noble knight Sir Tristram as he sat harping before his lady la Belle Isolde."
*The Boy's King Arthur* 1922 N. C. Wyeth illustrator

## First Tale
## The Tale of Arthur's Sword Excalibur

n his adventurous youth Arthur became king, but he hadn't a good sword, and without a good sword no king can amount to much. The best swords were forged by magic or acquired by a miracle, and Arthur, starting out with a blade of ordinary manufacture, nearly met his death. When he was fighting with Pellinore, his cheap weapon broke in pieces, and Pellinore would have cut off his head if Merlin hadn't happened along and engaged him in conversation. Pellinore, who liked to finish one thing at a time, wouldn't talk until Arthur was dead, so Merlin put an enchantment on him and told Arthur they'd better get out of there.

But Arthur was worried; they were sure to meet someone, and anyone you meet is likely to be an enemy, and he had no sword. Merlin said he knew of a sword in those parts which they might pick up as they rode along.

They came to a lake, broad and deep, and out of the middle of the water an arm rose up, waving a fine sword at them.

"Didn't I tell you?" said Merlin. "There's the sword now"

Before they could do anything about it they saw an engaging young woman walking on the water coming in their direction.

"Who is she?" asked Arthur.

"That's the Lady of the Lake" said Merlin, "she spends most of her time in a palace under a rock, which is under the surface and if you speak to her politely she will give you the sword".

Arthur put on his best manners. "Damsel, I need a sword, and that one would suit me perfectly if I could get it"

"Sir Arthur," said the lady, "it belongs to me but it's yours on one condition; promise me a little gift which I shall name later."

"Whatever you wish," replied Arthur, who could be reckless at times.

"Well," said the young woman," since you probably can't walk on water the way I can, seat yourself on yonder boat and row to where the sword is, and when you get to it, seize it firmly by the hilt and be sure to take the scabbard along. You'll need it."

"And what about that gift you spoke of?" said Arthur whose mind was beginning to work.

"Let me ask for that," said the damsel, "when the right time comes."

Arthur and Merlin got down and hitched their horses to a tree, and sat in the boat, Arthur doing the rowing. When they reached the hand sticking out of the water, he grasped the sword by the handle and gave a good pull. It came away more easily than he expected, and the scabbard with it, and at once the arm and the hand sank out of sight. He laid the sword reverently on the boat bottom and turned around to thank the lady, but she was gone.

So they made for shore, unhitched their horses and rode off, talking of this and that.

"Which do you fancy more", said Merlin, "the blade or the scabbard?"

"The blade, of course," said Arthur, perplexed that even a philosopher should ask a question as easy to answer as that.

"It's a matter of opinion," said Merlin. "The blade is out of the ordinary, but so is the sheath. So long as you have it strapped to your middle you won't bleed a drop, however you may be wounded."

Arthur's gratitude doubled at the news, and he promised never to leave the scabbard at home.

But though he had now found a sword worthy of him, the story isn't finished, as you can see for yourself; in the back of his head he was thinking the lady might put in an appearance any moment and ask something quite awkward. Besides, he had forgotten to inquire what the sword was called. The best swords, the magical ones, always have a name, and unless you know its name you can't get out of a sword what you should.

In those days it was, you might say, the fashion for damsels from faeryland to distribute magical weapons among the deserving. Arthur's case was not unique. To be sure, not all of the young women were as beautiful as the Lady of the Lake, few of them had skill in walking on water, and the swords they supplied couldn't match the quality of Arthur's, but that is easily understood. From the day of his birth he was a distinguished man.

One morning, when he was holding court at Camelot, in came one of those damsels, not the Lady of the Lake, but important in her own right. She had on a coat with fur trimmings, and a belt over that, and from the belt hung a noble sword.

"I'm astonished," said Arthur, "to see a woman so fiercely armed."

"No fault of mine," said she, "I must be cumbered with this weapon till I meet a man strong enough to pull it from its scabbard, and he should be not only strong, but saintly, which makes it hard."

Arthur turned to his barons and urged them to try, and though he bade only those who were good as well as muscular, the sword stayed where it was. Then up stepped Balin, a youth from Northumberland whose background was troubled and obscure. In one hand he gripped the scabbard, in the other the hilt, and out came the blade.

At that moment, of all times, appeared the Lady of the Lake, now on horseback.

"You're the one I want to see," said Arthur, helping her out of the saddle. "You didn't tell me the name of my sword."

"The name is Excalibur," she said. "Cut-steel is a free translation."

"An excellent name, that," Arthur said.

"I've come for my gift," she declared.

"Whatever you like," he replied.

"You may give me the head of the young man who has just won the sword, or the head of the damsel who brought it to him, or I shouldn't mind if you gave me both their heads. He killed my brother; she murdered my father."

"Of the damsel I know nothing," said Arthur, "but the young man two minutes ago demonstrated the soundness of his character."

"I want his head!"

"This is embarrassing," said Arthur. "Ask something else."

"Nothing else!"

Balin, standing by, was annoyed. "Is it my head you're asking for?"

"You heard correctly," said she.

With that he whipped out his new sword and trimmed the head off the Lady of the Lake as neatly as you'd clip a blossom from its stalk.

"For shame," said Arthur. "That's something you shouldn't have done!"

"Sir," said Balin," she was no friend of my family."

"That may be," said Arthur, "but I was in her debt and you shouldn't have killed her with me looking on."

Then Balin went his way, taking the lady's head with him and Arthur ordered a funeral for what was left of the Lady of the Lake. The lamentations were grievous, and the court wore mourning for the usual period, or a little longer.

## WHO WAS KING ARTHUR?

Arthur was a legendary king who was supposed to have ruled England in the 6th century. His father was King Uther Pendragon, and his mother Queen Igraine, who was wooed away from her first husband, the Duke of Tintagel, to become Queen of England. They died when Arthur was a lad and his training was entrusted to Merlin, who was a sorcerer.

Arthur surrounded himself with a company of valiant warriors named The Knights of the Round Table, who were supposed to restore order to Britain. Their remarkable adventures were first chronicled by Sir Thomas Malory, a Yorkshire scholar, who flourished in the 16th century. The sources of his material were believed to have been a series of verses written by the French troubadour, Chrétien de Troyes, in the 12th century, who may possibly have read about Arthur and his knights in the ancient Latin histories of Britain.

Published February 4, 1940

## Second Tale
## The Tale of Sir Tristam and the Love Potion

ing Anguish of Ireland had a daughter, La Beale Isoud, a fine girl and well brought up. Her mother taught her to mix poisons and behave in company.

It happened that King Anguish needed gold, so he put a tax on King Mark of Cornwall, who wished he had thought of it first, being short of cash himself.

"Sorry I am to be so poor", said he- which was true enough.

"Sorrow is common to us all," said the Irishman. "When may I expect the gold?"

"You may expect it from now on", said Mark.

Then King Anguish sent his wife's brother, Sir Marhaus, to collect the tax, and the Queen and La Beale Isoud put a drop of poison on the tip of his spear and the edge of his sword, so that he would be remembered.

Now Mark had a nephew, Sir Tristram, a large bony youth who played the harp and was appreciated by the ladies. The boy had gifts, but as yet was unreliable.

"Will somebody tell me," said King Mark," where I'm to lay hands on this money?"

"What money?", said Tristram, with his feet on a bench, harping as he talked.

"Will you stop that noise!" said Mark. "Sir Marhaus is come for my gold or my head."

"You need only one guess at that riddle," said Tristram, "since you have no gold."

"You're the family pest," said Mark, "and I don't know what my sister, your mother, was thinking of".

"Why not kill Marhaus", said Tristram," before he kills you?"

"That's the advice", said Mark, "that myself would give it to another man"

Tristram rested his harp on a peg on the wall. "Is the grindstone in working order?" said he.

"How should I know?" said Mark.

"Come along with me," said Tristram, "I'll show you how to put an edge on steel."

When the sword was sharpened he waved it up and down and crosswize, and asked for a hair out of Mark's red beard, and Mark pulled one for him. Then he blew the hair against the sword-edge and the hair was cut in half.

"Now don't let me waste my time," said Tristram. "Where's Marhaus?"

When Marhaus saw Tristram coming, he said, "Why should a boy like you fight a man like me?"

"The occasion is public," said Tristram, "and the audience is large. I'm somewhat behind in my reputation, but if I last out the afternoon, I'll be years ahead."

"It's a dastardly thing to send children to the wars," said Marhaus. "I'll leave that face of yours alone so the sexton will be able to tell just who he is burying."

First they tried spears, and each pushed the other off his horse, but Tristram had his side torn by the tip of the spear La Beale Isoud had poisoned. Then they drew swords and walloped as they might, blade ringing on blade or sinking into flesh, till the grass beneath them was red. Then Tristram remembered that if he didn't kill Marhaus before Marhaus killed him, Mark would have the laugh. He struck so hard, the sword went through the helmet and skull and into the brain-pan and he tugged three times before he could draw it out. Then he examined the blade, to see if he must grind it again, and he saw that he had nicked a piece out of it, like a half moon, which grieved him.

Then King Anguish buried Sir Marhaus, but first the Queen and La Beale Isoud went over his wounds, out of curiosity, to know what he died of, and they found sticking in his brain-pan a half-moon of steel, which they kept for a souvenir.

But Tristram went to bed with his poison. "Nephew, " said Mark, "to see you in health again I'd give all my gold."

Tristram smiled as broad a smile as he could, being weak.

"They who made the poison", said Mark, "should know the answer to it." Why don't you consult King Anguish's women?"

"They'd be prejudiced", said Tristram.

"When did they ever see you?", said Mark. "You can always change your name."

"I might call myself Tramtrist," said Tristram.

"It's an inspiration", said Mark. "They'd have to be smarter than I am to see through that."

When Tristram knocked at the palace door, they asked him in, though they were wearing black.

"Were you ever in Cornwall, Tramtrist?" said Anguish, off hand.

"Cornwall?", said Tristram, "where's that?"

"Where Marhaus was murdered," said Anguish. "Let me meet him who did it."

"I was wounded myself," said Tristram, "defending a lady."

"You fought in a good cause," said Anguish, who was a glutton for dust in the eye, "My wife will fix you up."

They put him to bed and the Queen said it was an interesting case, and La Beale Isoud said so too. In no time he was cured but he stayed a month longer because Isoud was in love with him and he didn't mind.

But one day he thought of taking a bath, so they heated the water, and while he was in the tub Isoud looked his cloths over, to be sure they didn't need mending, and there was a chip out of his sword, the match of what had stuck in Marhaus's brain-pan.

The Queen thought they should knife him before he got out of the tub, and the King thought it would look better if they let him put his clothes on, but La Beale Isoud said you couldn't execute a guest, not during his first visit.

"You're in rare luck," said Anguish, as they were saying good-bye. "Wait till I meet you on neutral ground!"

La Beale Isoud swore in his ear that she would love only him forever, and he swore the same in hers, being a gentleman.

Back in Cornwall, remembering the girl now and then, he spoke of her as one of the best he had met, until at last Mark began to think.

"If I marry her myself," said he, "and the tax can stay in the family, and you're the one to take Anguish the offer, since you know the way."

"Her parents dislike me," said Tristram.

"It's not you she's to marry," said Mark.

So Tristram visited Anguish a second time, and the King and his wife thought it was too much, and when he told his errand the King said Mark was sensible about the tax, and the Queen admitted a girl should have a husband, and Mark was perhaps better than nothing. La Beale Isoud looked pale.

"Take this bottle with you," said her mother. "It's a stirrup cup for you and Mark at your wedding. If you drink enough of it you will like each other."

But before they reached Cornwall Isoud and Tristram emptied the bottle, and there are folk who say their love was perfect ever after.

"Do I need to marry Mark now?", said Isoud.

"You wouldn't fly in the face of society, would you?", said Tristram. "They expect you to marry him".

"It's you I love," said Isoud.

"Don't I know it," said Tristram. "But your marriage won't interfere and it probably won't be permanent. Take a chance and see what happens."

## WHO WAS SIR TRISTRAM?

Tristram was the son of Meliodas, lord and king of the country of Liones, who married Elizabeth, sister of King Mark of Cornwall. Just before Tristram was born, his father was decoyed from home by an enchantress, and his mother, while searching the forest for him, gave birth to Tristram and died.

Meliodas married again but his second wife, a daughter of King Howell of Brittany, was jealous of Tristram and tried to poison him. The lad survived and his adventurous life began. He was brought up by a French tutor named Gouvernail who taught him to play the harp and hunt with a hawk. He could also play a notedly good game of chess and speak a number of foreign tongues.

After a while he went to live with his uncle Mark and he was a part-time member of King Arthur's Knights of the Round Table. His love for La Beale Isoud, or the beautiful Isoud, made the couple the most famous sweethearts in all medieval literature. Their romance was translated into many languages and almost all of the Western nations had their own version of the story. Richard Wagner used a typically German version, founded upon a poem by Gottfried von Strasberg his musical drama *"Tristram and Isolde"*.

In this country Edward Arlington Robinson's narrative poem "Tristram" is noteworthy, and to this company of distinguished interpreters of the old legend is now added Mr. John Erskine who retells it delightfully for readers of *The American Weekly*.

Published February 11, 1940

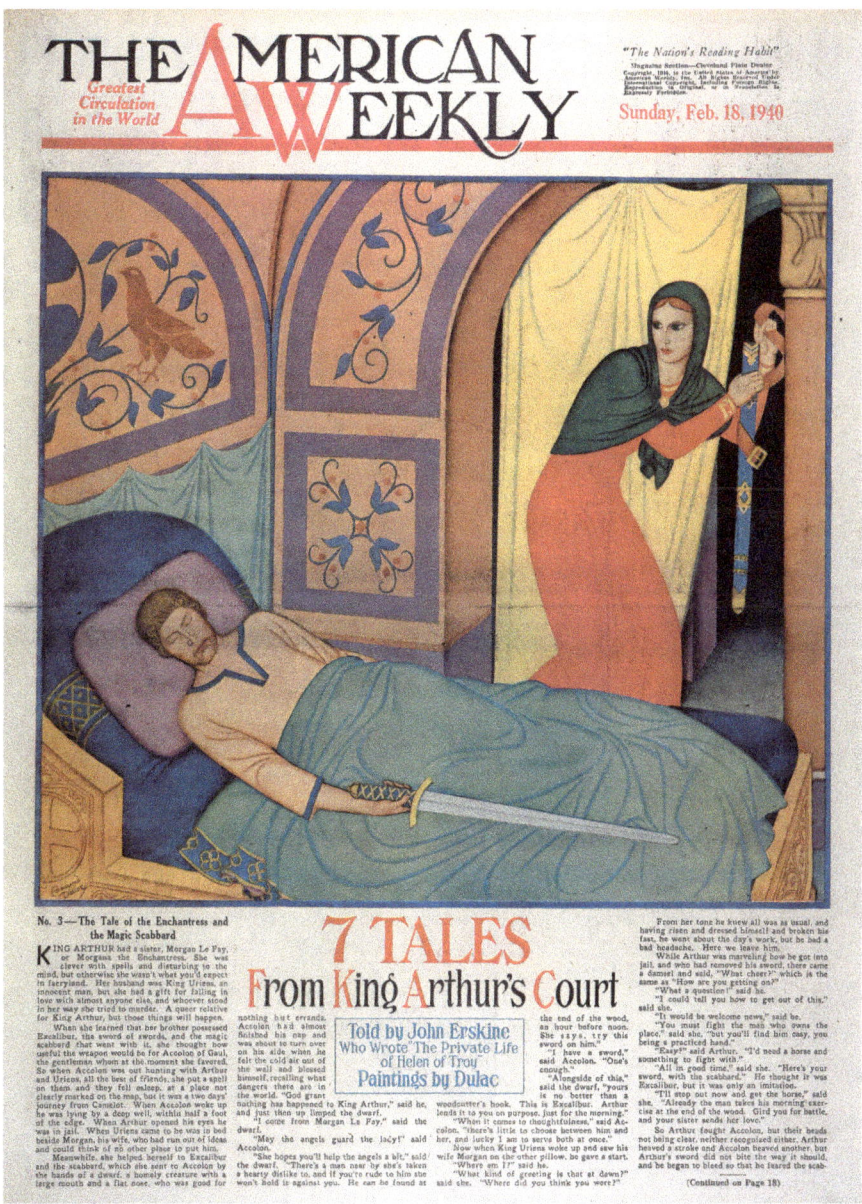

## Third Tale
## The Tale of the Enchantress and the Magic Scabbard

 ing Arthur had a sister, Morgan La Fay, or Morgana the Enchantress. She was clever with spells and disturbing to mind, but otherwise she wasn't what you'd expect in faeryland. Her husband was King Uriens, an innocent man, but she had a gift for falling in love with almost anyone else, and whoever stood in her way she tried to murder.

When she learned that her brother possessed Excalibur, the sword of swords, and the magic scabbard that went with it, she thought how useful the weapon would be for Accolon of Gaul, the gentleman, whom at the moment she favored. So when Accolon was out hunting with Arthur and Uriens, all the best of friends, she put a spell on them and they fell asleep, at a place not clearly marked on a map, but it was a two days journey from Camelot. When Accolon woke up he was lying by a deep well, within half a foot of the edge. When Arthur opened his eyes he was in jail. When Uriens opened his eyes he was in bed beside Morgan, his wife, who had run out of ideas and could think of no other place to put him.

Meanwhile, she helped herself to Excalibur and the scabbard, which she sent to Accolon by the hands of a dwarf, a homely creature with a large mouth and a flat nose, who was good for nothing but errands. Accolon has almost finished his nap and was about to turn over on his side when he felt the cold air coming out of the well and blessed himself, recalling what dangers there are in the world. "God grant nothing has happened to King Arthur," said he, and just then up limped the dwarf.

"I come from Morgan La Fay," said the dwarf.

"May the angels guard the lady," said Accolon.

"She hopes you'll help the angels a bit," said the dwarf.

"There's a man nearby she's taken a hardy dislike to, and if you're rude to him she won't hold that against you. He can be found at the end of the wood, an hour before noon. She says try this sword on him."

"I have a sword," said Accolon, "One's enough."

"Alongside of this," said the dwarf, "yours is no better than a woodcutter's hook. This is Excalibur. Arthur lends it to you on purpose, just for the morning."

"When it comes to thoughtfulness," said Accolon," there is little to choose between him and her, and lucky I am to serve both at once."

Now when King Uriens woke up and saw his wife Morgan on the other pillow, he gave a start.

"Where am I?" said he.

"What kind of greeting is that at dawn?" said she. "Where did you think you were?"

From her tone he knew all was as usual, and having risen and dressed himself and broken his fast, he went about the day's work, but he had a bad headache. Here we leave him.

While Arthur was marveling how he got into jail, and who had removed his sword, there came a damsel who said "What cheer?", which is the same as "How are you getting on?"

"What a question!" said he.

"I could tell you how to get out of this," said she.

"It would be welcome news," said he.

"You must fight the man who owns the place," said she, "but you'll find him easy, you being a practiced hand."

"Easy?" said Arthur. "I'd need a horse and something to fight with."

"All in good time," said she. "Here is your sword with the scabbard." He thought it was from Excalibur, but it was only an imitation.

"I'll step out now and get the horse," said she. "Already the man takes his morning exercise at the end of the wood. Gird you for battle, and your sister sends her love."

So Arthur fought Accolon, but their heads not being clear, neither recognized either. Arthur heaved a stroke and Accolon heaved another, but Arthur's sword did not bite the way it should and he began to bleed so that he feared the scabbard wasn't working.

"Now", said Accolon, "brace yourself for this one!". With that he whaled Arthur all but off his horse.

"It's your turn to brace," said Arthur, lashing out. Those who saw the fight agreed there was never a champion as game as Arthur, considering how much he bled.

Then Arthur took time out but Accolon hit when he wasn't looking.

"What kind of fight is this?", said Arthur. And straightaway broke his sword on Accolon's head. Then he knew that the sword was not good, and with both hands he seized his shield by the rim and dented Accolon's skull.

"Sir," said Accolon, "you'll be bled white. Do you give up?"

"The way this battle is going," said Arthur, "I'd rather be in my place than yours; to fight without a sword adds to my reputation, but if you kill me when I'm unarmed, it won't count."

Then Accolon led with a fierce thrust and once more drew blood, but Arthur pounded with the shield till he gave ground, and pounded again, so that Accolon dropped Excalibur, and Arthur leaned adroitly from his horse and picked it up. Straightaway his fingers recognized the hilt, but to make sure, he tested the blade on Accolon's thigh where the flesh was thick, and he nearly sliced off the belt, where hung the scabbard of Excalibur.

"Did you repeat your prayers this morning?" said he, sweeping such a cut that Accolon began to bleed wherever he could.

"I doubt", said Accolon, "I could be killed by a better man."

"Your politeness," said Arthur, "is extraordinary. Who are you?"

"One of King Arthur's men", said Accolon.

"So am I", said the King. "In fact, I'm Arthur himself."

"Can it be?", said Accolon, amazed.

"It is," said Arthur.

Then was Accolon so sorry he began to cry.

"Save your tears," said Arthur. "We'll get you to a doctor before it's too late."

But Accolon dies shortly, for want of care, the doctor being out on another case. So Arthur put the corpse on a horse-bier and gave command to six knights who were free at the moment, "Take it to that sister of mine and say I send her a present."

He himself, needing sleep, rested in the first house he came to.

Morgan La Fay waited for news of the fight.

"Out with it!", she cried, when the dwarf pushed his flat nose through the doorway.

"He's dead," said the dwarf.

"Well, I never liked him," said she.

"Are we talking of the same person?" said the dwarf.

"Don't tell me Accolon was hurt!" said she.

"Wasn't he though!", said the dwarf.

Then she rode where Arthur was sleeping, and would have stolen Excalibur, but he slept with the naked sword in his right hand, and she feared to disturb him. So she carried off the scabbard, thinking it better than nothing, and rode home thoughtful.

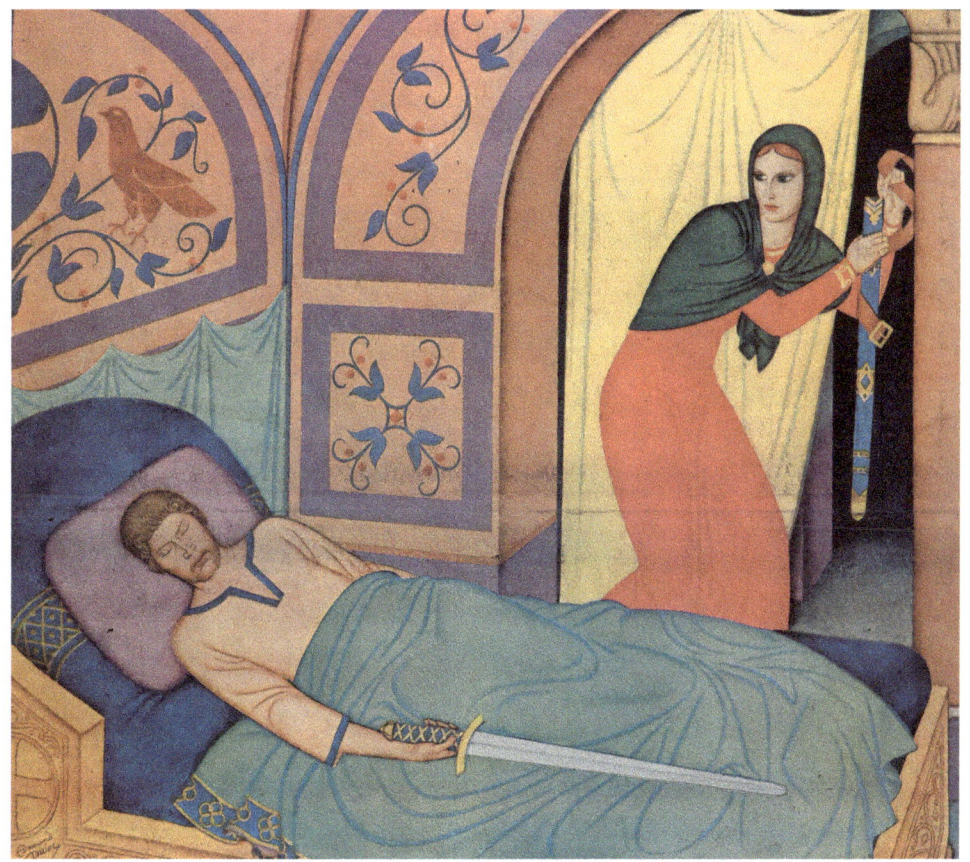

## WHO WAS MORGAN LA FAY?

Morgan La Fay was one of King Arthur's sisters and married King Uriens of North Wales. She and her husband possessed magic powers, according to the old legends, and used them whenever they could. Morgan was called "La Fay", which means "The Fairy" or "The Enchantress", not because she was dainty or could fly with wings, but because she could things other ordinary mortals couldn't.

Morgan disliked Arthur for most of her life and was always thinking up new deviltry to annoy him. She tried to kill her brother by means of Accolon, as Mr. Erskine relates. When this failed she did all she could to get rid of her husband Uriens, but he was saved by his son Sir Uwaine.

Morgan spent part of her charmed life underwater when she assumed the form of one of The Ladies of the Lake. On these vacations she would lure knights into her caves and give them valuable presents when she was finished with them.

Her story was a famous one in medieval times and well known in Italy. Her name was given to a mirage often seen at sea on the coast of Calabria. Sailors called it "Fata Morgana" after Morgan La Fay. In Denmark, where Morgan was also supposed to have lived, she fell in love with the hero, Ogier, when he was one hundred years old. She rejuvenated him and they lived together for two hundred years.

Published February 18, 1940

## Fourth Tale
## The Tale of Sir Galahad and His Quest for the Sangreal

hey say that Joseph of Aramathie brought to England, in a precious cup, the living blood-the Sangreal-of Christ. So long as Arthur and his Round Table served God, the Sangreal revealed itself to their fellowship, but when their fellowship was shattered by sin, the Sangreal disappeared, and the best of Arthur's knights went in search of it. Sir Lancelot joined the quest, deeply troubled at heart, since he and Queen Guinevere had supplied most of the sin, but there were younger knights whose souls were clean-Sir Percivale and Sir Bors-and Sir Galahad, the purest of all.

Sir Galahad may have seemed, though admirable, a little peculiar, for though he was a saint, there is no mention of his having cared much for the men and women he met; if there was one thing he liked more than another it was to avoid human society and disappear over the horizon. But some things that happened to him just at the end will make all clear, especially nowadays when the human race is not behaving well, and you and I might envy Sir Galahad his privilege of quitting when he had enough.

He loved his father, Sir Lancelot, and admired him so far as it was practicable, but he knew of course why his father couldn't find the Sangreal. Sir Lancelot indeed came pretty near it; he reached a house where for the moment the Sangreal adobe, and an old hermit was in charge of it, and maybe it was an angel disguised as a hermit, and the angel said Sir Lancelot would be admitted to the heavenly vision if first he confessed his sins in true penitence. He confessed everything, including Queen Guinevere.

"And do you repent?", said the angel.

"I do," said Sir Lancelot, but then being honest held up a finger. "Wait a moment, what do you mean by repent?"

"To repent," said the angel, "is to be sorry, to wish you had never done it, and you'll never do it again."

"When I say repent," said Lancelot, "I mean I'm sorry it was a sin."

"That's repentance in the abstract," said the angel to Lancelot.

"Must I be sorry," asked Sir Lancelot, "that I loved her and she loved me?"

"You must," said the angel.

Lancelot thought it over, then with a great pain in his heart got up off his knees and left the house.

This was of course a grief to Sir Galahad, but it had been going on for some time, and though he would never be used to it, it was nothing new. He and Sir Percivale and Sir Bors continued the quest without Sir Lancelot's help. After tiresome wanderings they reached a castle in which was a friend of theirs, King Pelles and his son Eliazar. While they were talking of this and that they heard a voice say, "Two among you are not looking for the Sangreal, and therefore must leave." King Pelles and his son left.

Then to Galahad, Percivale and Bors appeared five angles from Heaven, and a man who looked like a bishop. This man was Joseph of Aramathie, who greeted them and gave his blessing. And he showed them the Sangreal.

The peace in their hearts was such as they had never known before, especially Galahad. In that moment of exaltation he made a strange prayer; he asked that he might die promptly whenever he should say the word, and a voice from Heaven assured him he'd have his request.

Then Joseph gave them the Sangreal to carry through the world. Wherever there was sickness or distress, and hearts ready to receive the blessing, the Sangreal brought healing, beginning with a minor king, who had trouble with his legs.

They came at least to the city of Sarras, which is not definitely located, but it was a large city and a strong king governed it whose name was Estorause. He didn't like foreigners and sought to keep his people to themselves. Oddly enough, his people were mostly lame.

When Galahad, Percivale and Bors approached the city carrying the Sangreal and a silver table they usually rested it on, they met a crooked old man, and Galahad asked him to help with the silver table since it was heavy.

"Bless me," said the old man," For ten years now these crutches have been all I could handle. Besides, you have with you two able knights."

"Never mind that", said Galahad "Do your best and show your good will."

The old man put his hand to the table, and immediately was as sound as ever he'd been. When the procession had moved into the city, Galahad, lifting one side of the table and the cured cripple managing the other, the news of the miracle spread, and the common folk were happier than they had long been, saying to each other that now the good old times might return. But when King Estorause heard of it, he asked Galahad and his companions where they came from and what they had brought on the silver table. When he learned it was the Sangreal he put them in jail, he being a dictator with his own religion.

You might suppose that Galahad would have asked to die then, but it wasn't danger he ever turned his back on. He and his companions languished in their cell till King Estorause fell mortally sick and sent for them, and they put him in the way of grace, yet they were careful to perform no miracles, therefore he died.

Then the people of the city by unanimous vote elected Galahad King. None knew better than he that holding office is bad for the soul, so he declined. But they insisted, and because he hoped, with the aid of the Sangreal, to do much good, at last he said he'd try.

But at the end of the year, though he was still himself, the ordeal had been heavy, and he had seen what becomes of men who go into politics, those who are not saints like Galahad.

Then he took farewell of Percival and Bors, and he asked Bors to bear a message to Sir Lancelot, his father, and the message was that Lancelot should reflect how unstable was the world, and though he meant Guinevere, he didn't name her, being a gentleman. Then he knelt down at the table and prayed, reminding heaven of its promise, and the angels came for him.

## WHO SIR GALAHAD WAS, AND WHAT THE QUEST FOR THE SANGREAL WAS

Sir Galahad was the son of Sir Lancelot and Elaine, the daughter of King Pelles, a cousin of Joseph of Aramathie. As a youth, Galahad was brought up by an aged hermit and had no contact with worldly things. His guardian brought him to King Arthur's court to become a knight of the Round Table. At this table was a vacant seat, called the "Siege Perilous" destined for the knight who would seek the Holy Grail, or The Sangreal.

The Holy Grail signified, in the medieval legends, the chalice used by the Saviour at the Last Supper, in which Joseph of Aramathie received the Saviour's blood- the Sangreal- at the Cross. Joseph was supposed to have brought the Grail with him to England and the knights resolved to go in search of it. Galahad took his seat in the "Siege Perilous", and as the knights vowed to seek the Grail, the hermit Naciens warned them that only one who was clean of sin could find it.

One by one the knights dropped out until only Galahad was left. He received a vision of the Grail and then the Grail itself at Carbonek Castle. He became King of Sarras, as Mr. Erskine relates, and finally died. The Grail was borne to heaven by the angels and, says the legend, was never seen again.

There are many variations of the tale of the quest for the Grail. Perhaps the most famous is the legend concerning Perceval, immortalized by Richard Wagner in his religious pageant and music drama, "Parsifal". Tennyson used the theme in "Idylls of the King" and now Mr. Erskine tells the story in his own delightful way.

Published February 25, 1940

## Fifth Tale
## The Tale of Lancelot and the Four Queens

hen Sir Lancelot was young, he needed adventures, and every so often he went out to see what he could find. On the day we now speak of he took with him his nephew, Sir Lionel, who was still younger, and together they rode until they came to a wood, about noon. Then, for a whim, Sir Lancelot would rather have a nap than an adventure, and straightaway, he descended from his horse and stretched himself under an apple tree.

"Lionel," said he, "call me if anyone comes."

So, crossing one ankle over the other and clasping his hands on his chest, he slept, while Lionel paced up and down, inquiring of himself what kind of adventure is this.

Then he saw three knights running, one behind the other, and after them a fourth, a powerful gentleman who caught up with one after the other, served them a knock on the head, and draped them like sacks over their own saddles, bound hand and foot with the reins of their own bridles. He was leading them off in a pack-horse line when it occurred to Sir Lionel that here was an adventure if he were quick about it. So, he tip-toed to his own horse, not to awaken Lancelot, and having mounted, set his spear in rest and charged at the oversized knight who had just stunned three in a row. Thereupon the large knight, with no trouble at all, served Sir Lionel also a knock, picked him up and hung him over the saddle like the others, hitched him to the end of the procession, and led the train down the road.

Meanwhile Sir Lancelot slept one of the best naps that ever he slept till the sun reached his face and might have roused him had not four ladies come riding near the apple tree. They were Queens of great estate, all four, and beautiful, yet in character they were not much. One was Queen of Northgalis, and one was Queen of Eastland, and one was Queen of Out Isles, wherever those places may be, and one was Arthur's sister-Morgan La Fay, which throws light on the others.

Seeing Lancelot asleep under the bough with his ankles crossed and his hands folded, the four ladies fell in love with him, though at the moment his mouth was open, and each last plotted how to dispose of her three friends.

"Don't let's quarrel," said Morgan La Fay, who saw things in the large. "He's not enough for four, but we can't multiply him by losing our tempers. We'll put an enchantment on him and take him home. One of the rooms has bars on the windows. When his brain clears, in six hours or five, let him choose."

"Why not draw lots?" said the Queen of the Out Isles, who had small trust in Morgan. "I'd leave it to chance."

"Let a man choose his love," said Morgan, "and you've left it indeed to chance, for no man has sense. It may well be he'll choose you."

Thereupon the Queen of the Out Isles smiled and said Morgan had a pretty wit, and Morgan smiled back so you would think of arsenic. Then they ceased from pleasantry, the sun being already in Lancelot's eye, so they put the spell on him and took him home, and occupied themselves till he slept it off.

Then came again those four Queens, more beautiful than before, having used the time to work on their faces.

"Sir Knight," said they, "what cheer?"-as though to ask, "How do you feel now?"

"Ladies," said Lancelot, "I'd know how I felt if I knew where I was."

The Queen of the Out Isles would have spoken, but Morgan La Fay waved a hand for silence.

"I'll tell him," said she," since this is my house and the words come easy. Sir Lancelot, you are in love."

"Did I talk in my sleep?", said Lancelot with a start, "I promised Guinevere I'd tell nobody."

"You're in love with us," said Morgan, "and we'll be glad to know which it is."

Bewildered, he stared at them all four standing as straight as they could and breathing deep for effect. He was interested but he shook his head.

"I don't think so," said he, "I believe it's still Guinevere."

"Absurd," said the Queen of the Out Isles.

"I'm speaking to him," said Morgan. "Lancelot, you can't have Guinevere and she can't have you."

"Who says I can't?"

"I say so," broke in the Queen of Northgalis. Morgan gave her a look.

"You ladies are very kind," said Lancelot, "but this is my business."

Then Morgan raised her finger, as often she did, for emphasis. "Lancelot," said she, "you may give your love to one of us, and you had best be quick about it, or you may be a dead man."

"Is it die or marry one of you?" said Lancelot in a sarcastic tone. "Never had I a choice where there was so little to choose."

Then were the four ladies astonished. "Is this your answer?" said they.

"Which?" said Lancelot.

"Do you refuse us?"

"You have it right," said Lancelot. "One by one and all together you are refused."

Then three of the ladies looked at Morgan Le Fe and she was in doubt what to reply, expecting nothing so plain.

"Think it over," said she.

"There is no need," said he.

"Does any one form of death," said she, "appeal to you more than another?"

"Your mind runs on choices, doesn't it?", said Lancelot who was well-nigh exasperated.

Then the four Queens, out of self-respect, retired, and Lancelot, well rested after his napping, wretched apart the bars of the window and climbed free, and it happened that the ladies, full of loving thoughts, had neglected to remove his armor. Then he went to the stable and helped himself to his horse, Morgan's housekeeping being careless and the stable door open. Then when he tasted the evening air, with life before him, he sang for joy.

Out of a cottage window a woman stuck her head to ask who was making that din.

"Damsel," said Lancelot politely, "what cheer?"

"I thought I heard something," said she.

"Are there any good adventures around here?" said he.

"There's a good one up the road," said she, "one of the best. In yonder castle lives a knight somewhat touched in the head. He brings home unconscious gentlemen tied to their own saddles, and keeps them in the dungeon on bread and water, and each morning he pays them a visit and laughs at them, saying ha-ha.

Then Lancelot hurried to the castle, killed the crazy knight, unlocked the dungeon door and rebuked Lionel.

"You promised to wake me up", said he, "if anybody came."

"I expected to be gone but a moment", said Lionel.

"Let it be a lesson to you," said Lancelot. "I over-slept."

## WHO SIR LANCELOT WAS

Sir Lancelot was born the son of King Ban of Britany and was kidnapped in his youth by Vivienne, a Lady of the Lake who had magical powers. She kept him till he grew to manhood and sent him to Arthur's court. He became a knight of the Round Table and Arthur's most trusted henchman.

According to the old legends, Lancelot fell in love with Guinevere, Arthur's Queen, and remained faithful to her all his life. Their mutual affection caused trouble at Camelot and resulted in finally breaking up Arthur's kingdom and the Round Table.

The trouble began at a tournament at Winchester where Sir Lancelot met

Elaine, his host's daughter, who was known as the Fair Maid of Ascolot. She loved Lancelot and gave him her sleeve to wear at the joust for good luck. Lancelot was wounded and Elaine nursed him back to health. Gawaine, who liked to gossip, told all to Guinevere, much to her distress. When Lancelot recovered and returned to court Guinevere accused him and he left in anger. Elaine died of a broken heart and her body was put on a barge which floated down past Guinevere's window. Guinevere realized that Lancelot never returned Elaine's love and the pair made up.

Later on, Lancelot met the four Queens, including Morgan Le Fe, Arthur's clever sister. The Queen of Northgalis probably ruled over what is now Northern Wales, the Queen of Eastern governed the eastern counties of England and perhaps the Queen of the Out Isles held sway over the islands lying south of Britain. However lovely they may have been, or enchanting, Lancelot remained faithful to Guinevere as Mr. Erskine relates.

Published March 3, 1940

## Sixth Tale
## The Tale of Merlin and One of The Ladies of the Lake

hen King Arthur married Queen Guinevere he invited his Round Table to a feast, and Merlin, because he was advanced in years and wise, had charge of the arrangements and told each knight where he was to sit. The dinner was good but plain, and there were just chairs enough to go 'round.

Hardly were they seated and Arthur had begun to carve the roast, when in came a young woman, good looking but excited, and the knights who were nearest and therefore most hopeful, stood up with their napkins still in their hands, and moved their chairs closer to make room. But Guinevere noticed the girl's beauty and asked Arthur to explain.

"I can't recall who she is," said he, "though I may have met her somewhere."

"You may indeed!" said Guinevere in such a tone that Arthur saw his wedding might get out of hand.

"Were you looking for anyone?", said Arthur to the girl, as Merlin told the waiter to bring an extra chair.

"I was looking for you", said she.

"There's a mistake somewhere," said he.

"Several," said she, "and now's the time to right them."

"Now really," said Arthur, smiling in a sick way and trying to remember.

But before the girl could say more a burley knight burst into the hall, fully armed, and seized her by the elbow and waist and dragged her toward the door, and she screamed with the full strength of her lungs. So, he carried her off, and they of the Round Table inquired by glances, one of another, whether to rescue her, with the Queen feeling as she did.

"There", said Arthur, "I'm glad she's gone. Wasn't she noisy?"

"Go on with your carving," said Guinevere.

Then the waiter brought the extra chair that Merlin had commanded, and Merlin, with his eyes still full of the girl, forgot he was old.

"Have I seen what I thought I saw? "said he.

"What was it like?", said Arthur.

"A guest wrenched from your dinner table, and you watching."

"I didn't consider her a guest," said Arthur, "because I didn't invite her."

"Was she in your dining room, or wasn't she?" said Merlin.

"I'll do whatever you advise," said Arthur," but no one asked her to come."

"Let Pellinore fetch her back", said Merlin.

"What do you think?", said the King, looking at his wife.

"Pellinore should have his dinner first," said Guinevere.

"I can't eat when a lady's in danger," said Pellinore, pushing his chair back.

So Pellinore armed himself and mounted his horse, and the night being dark and he doubtful which of several roads to take, he counted so in a child's game and so chose. In the morning he met a poor man in a valley, a laborer who took the world as it is, not being well bred.

"Fellow," said Pellinore, "did a gentleman pass this way hauling a lady by the elbow and waist?".

"A gentleman passed," said the man," but he wasn't hauling anything."

"Was he alone?"

"He was not," said the fellow," a lady was with him."

"Collect your wits," said Pellinore." Did she scream?"

"Not at first", said the man. "They came riding calm as two cows, grazing into the wind, but then another gentleman showed himself 'round the bend. That's when she screamed."

"Go on," said Pellinore. "What happened?"

"Let me see," said the fellow, scratching the back of his head. "As I recollect, he asked her- the new gentleman- if she needed a rescue, and she said she did, and the first gentleman thought the road here was too narrow, so they all went over to the meadow."

"Where's the meadow?", said Pellinore.

The man raised his arm to point. "You go a fair piece straight ahead, then turn to the right."

When Pellinore came to the meadow the knights were slashing and the blood was streaking their armor with red, and the lady was sitting under the hedge, looking pleased.

"I'll fight you both, one at a time", cried Pellinore, and they left off their battle to see who it was, and by the pattern of his helmet Pellinore knew the knight who had torn the lady from Arthur's table, so he raised his sword and split his skull.

"Now you next," he said to the other.

"I believe I shan't fight any more this morning," said the other. It's violent exercise and I need my strength for the journey."

Then Pellinore helped the lady into her saddle, and they rose toward

Camelot. He thought her a trifle less beautiful than she seemed before.

"How can I thank you?" said she.

"Don't," said he.

"But I'd like to," said she.

"I'd rather you didn't," said he.

After a while she smiled at him, as if sharing a pleasant thought. "That makes two rescues in one day."

Pellinore stuck his spur into his horse, to avoid answering.

"I haven't heard your name," said the lady.

"It's rarely mentioned," said he.

"What is it?"

"Pellinore."

"You don't know mine," said she.

"No," said he.

"I am Nimue, one of the Ladies of the Lake."

He spurred his horse again.

"Don't ride so fast," said she. "There's a soft spot of grass and I want to get down and rest."

"You'll make us late," said he.

Then they dismounted, and she stretched herself on the grass, and he propped himself on his elbow, chewing a green blade. Then he saw she was still wide awake, with her eyes on him.

"Didn't you say you wanted to rest?".

"I did not."

Then he saw she was untruthful and they mounted their horses and came to Camelot.

"That woman," said Merlin "will be my undoing."

"Don't you think," said Arthur, "you're too old?"

"Old enough to be her grandfather," said Merlin, "but I see what's going to happen."

"If you know it in advance," said Arthur, "you can take precautions."

"So you think," said Merlin.

Thereafter it came true, as he said, and Nimue spent much time with him, but in such a manner as though she were resigned.

"Now, you're a wise man," said she. "Why do none at Camelot seek my company but only you?"

For reply, he asked for her love, and she, changing the subject, said she wished she knew magic, and he said the simplest experiment for a beginner was with rocks, like the one sticking out of Camelot lawn. So he taught her the enchantment for raising and lowering rocks, and having raised it she asked, "Do you see my handkerchief anywhere?" and while he was looking she lowered the rock on top of him and went her ways.

Then Arthur, with grief in his voice, told Guinevere what had happened, and she listened as though she knew it in advance.

"Yet," said he, "Merlin was the wisest of us all."

"That may well be," said his wife.

## WHO MERLIN WAS

Merlin's birth and parenthood are doubtful, according to the many old legends in which he figured. In one, he is known as Ambrosius, a boy without mortal parents, who interprets an omen for the British King Vortigern and helps him rout the enemy Saxons.

In another old story, he is the son of the devil, and helps Uther, Arthur's father, move the great stones to Stonehenge in England from Naas in Ireland.

When Arthur was a lad, Uther made Merlin his tutor, and later on, Merlin helped Arthur defeat his foes by magic. Merlin was supposed to have made the Round Table and taken Arthur to the lake where one of the ladies gave him the magic sword Excalibur.

The Ladies of the Lake are rather indistinct characters in the Arthurian legends. Nimue is the one who gave the sword to Arthur and is killed by Balin, one of the knights. Later on, she reappears and rescues Arthur from peril. She marries Pelleas and Merlin falls in love with her. She inveigles him under a rock, as Mr. Erskine relates. She is also one of the three Queens in the ship in which Arthur is born away after battle.

According to one authority, Nimue is merely one aspect of the mythical figure Morgan, the Lady of the Lake, who also appears as Morgan Le Fe, Arthur's sister. At one time she is benevolent as Nimue, at another malicious as Morgan. She is also spoken of as Vivien, but this mistake was made by early copyists of the old tales.

Tennyson wrote of Merlin and Vivien in his "Idylls of the King" although he preferred the version that Vivien induced Merlin to take refuge from a storm in an old oak tree and left him there spellbound. Shakespeare mentions Merlin in "King Lear" and in "Henry IV" and the general opinion is that Merlin was perhaps a god of ancient British mythology, especially worshipped at Stonehenge.

Published March 10, 1940

## Seventh Tale
## The Tale of How Sir Lancelot Slew Sir Argavaine

n the season of Spring, when the sap runs, the branch blossoms, and the heart stirs. Sir Agravaine bethought him to kill Sir Lancelot, to whom as it chanced had taken a dislike. So, he spoke to Sir Gawaine and several others in the corridor at Camelot, outside the King's chamber.

"Lancelot is bold," said he.

"You mean brave," said Gawaine.

"I mean Guinevere," said the other.

"Tell nothing about it," said Gawaine. "It's no concern of mine."

"I'm thinking of telling Arthur, "said Argavaine.

"You're likely to make trouble between him and Lancelot," said Gawaine," and you'll be popular with neither of them. And, it's the best Spring weather we've enjoyed for years," he added hastily, seeing the door open and King Arthur himself at the threshold.

"My lords," said he, "how many times have I asked you to make less noise?"

"Would you rather we kept on whispering?", said Agravaine.

"Whispering what?"

"That Lancelot is your wife's boyfriend."

"If this is true--" said the king, looking at it from all sides.

"It is," said Agravaine.

"Then tell me nothing about it," said the King. "It concerns me only indirectly."

"It offends me, if it doesn't you," said Agravaine.

"You shouldn't go around spreading rumors," said Arthur, not unless you have proof.

"My lord," said Agravaine, "do you call me a liar?"

"Far from it, far from it," said Arthur, but the evidence is weak."

"If we caught him and her making love, "said Agravaine, "would that be evidence?"

"The very best," said the King, "but it's too much to hope for."

"Do you hunt tomorrow?", said Agravaine?"

"All day," said Arthur.

"Does Lancelot go with you?", said Agravaine.

"No." The King looked bothered. "I believe he has another engagement."

"Take your cook with you," said Agravaine.

"Why the cook?", said the King.

"It gives the impression you're dining in the woods," said Agravaine. "You'll come home early, of course, and see what you see."

"I don't like your advice," said Arthur. "He's a dangerous man when provoked."

"I'll handle him with tact," said Agravaine.

In the morning Arthur rode on his hunt, having told the Queen he would probably be out all night, and as the day wore to a close, Lancelot dressed with special care, and Sir Bors asked him why, and he said it was a dinner engagement he had almost forgotten.

"You'd better dine with me," said Bors.

"But I promised to go," said Lancelot.

"If you'll listen to a friend, " said Bors, "you'll stay home now and then."

"It isn't like you to worry," said Lancelot.

"God bless you, since you won't be convinced," said Bors. "But come home early."

So Lancelot put on his best coat and put his sword under his arm, and stepped around to the Queens room, and as soon as she recognized his knock she let him in and bolted the door again. Then were the two together, talking of this and that, and for a while they were undisturbed.

But at last, Agravaine with twelve of his men banged on the door.

"Shall I come in," said he, "or will you come out?"

"I'm not coming out tonight," said Guinevere.

"I spoke to Lancelot," said Argavaine.

"This is embarrassing," said Guinevere softly.

"You don't happen to have a coat-of-mail or a shield, do you?" whispered Lancelot.

"Do you think they'll kill you?"

"I'm wondering if your husband will burn you at the stake."

"What an idea!" said she.

"If you live longer than I do," said he, "remember to pray for my soul."

"Oh, I shan't survive you," she said. "I couldn't bear it."

Then Lancelot kissed Guinevere, being deeply touched. "I'm sorrier for you than for myself, since I'm older and have missed little," he said.

"Open the door!" shouted Agravaine, pounding.

"You know," said Lancelot thoughtfully, "I could handle them easily if I had a horse and armor."

"But you haven't," said she.

"That is so," said he.

Then Argavaine and his fellows picked up a bench and began to ram the door.

"Who knocks?", called Lancelot, as though he heard them for the first time.

"He's in there," said Argavaine. "Give another heave with the settee."

"Are you trying to enter the Queen's boudoir?" called Lancelot.

"You tried first," said Argavaine.

"You'll have to prove it," said Lancelot.

"Here are a dozen witnesses," said Argavaine.

"I mean legal proof," said Lancelot, "on my body, in a fair fight"

Then he set open the door and Argavaine stepped in, and Sir Lancelot was waiting for him in his best coat, with his sword raised. Then he split Agravaine's head to the collarbone, and the other gentlemen departed, perceiving the incident closed.

"I'm thinking of leaving Camelot," said Lancelot to the Queen. "Would you care to go with me?"

"Would that look well?", asked the Queen. "Besides, Arthur likes to talk over the hunt afterwards.

"This is one of the best evenings I ever spent," said Lancelot, "until we were interrupted."

"Do you remember the time," said she, "when we lived simply and there was leisure?"

"We shouldn't quarrel with progress," said he. "The world moves on."

He kissed her and she kissed him, and each gave the other a ring, for remembrance. Then, having pulled Argavaine into the corridor so the door would shut, he strolled home through the May night, smelling the young blossoms on the branch, feeling the sap stirring, and lifting an eye to the stars which twinkled above the quiet world.

## WHO AGRAVAINE AND GUINEVERE WERE

Sir Argavaine was the son of King Lot of Orkney and Morgawse, a sister of King Arthur and Morgan Le Fay. He was the brother of Gawaine, Gaheris and Gareth. As King Arthur's nephew he felt it his duty to expose the love of Lancelot and Guinevere. Also, he was jealous of Lancelot's power at court.

Legends say that Guinevere was the daughter of a noble Roman family, brought up in the household of Cador, Duke of Cornwall. She suspected Lancelot of loving Elaine, the Fair Maid of Ascolot, but after Elain's death became reconciled to him.

From this point, Mr. Erskine picks up the story and relates how Agravaine and the twelve knights surprised the lovers. One of the knights was named Modred, who reported to the King. Lancelot escaped and later on the Queen joined him. Arthur and Gawaine, to avenge Agravaine, besieged Lancelot and the Queen in Launcelot's Castle *Joyous Gard*. Lancelot restored Guinevere to Arthur and retired to Brittany. While he was away, Modred attempted to seize his kingdom.

After several battles Modred retreated, but in the final battle, Modred and Arthur mortally wounded each other and Arthur was borne off to Avalon. Lancelot came back from Brittany to help Arthur win back his kingdom, but finding him dead, sought out Guinevere who had entered a convent.

Lancelot became a priest and stood guard over Arthur's grave. When Guinevere died she was buried with Arthur and, legends say, the abbey of Glastonbury rose over their graves. Lancelot died not long after and was carried to his castle *Joyous Gard*.

In Tennyson's "Idylls of the King" Arthur is said to have forgiven Guinevere, who, heartbroken and contrite, entered the convent at Alemsbury while Arthur went off to fight for his kingdom. In this way, the Arthurian legends close and the age of chivalry in England comes to an end.

Published March 17,1940

# FURTHER READING

WIKIPEDIA, the free online encyclopedia, has several entries for King Arthur.

*The Lady of Shalott* by Alfred, Lord Tennyson (1833)

*The Legends of King Arthur and His Knights* by James Knowles (1862)

*The Boy's King Arthur* by Sidney Lanier (1880)

*Tristram of Lyonesse* by Algernon Charles Swinburne (1882)

*Idylls of the King* by Alfred, Lord Tennyson (1859–1885)

*A Connecticut Yankee in King Arthur's Court* by Mark Twain (1889)

Howard Pyle - In a four-volume set including:

- o "The Story of King Arthur and His Knights" (1903)
- o "The Story of the Champions of the Round Table" (1905)
- o "The Story of Sir Launcelot and His Companions" (1907)
- o "The Story of the Grail and the Passing of King Arthur" (1910)

*The Once and Future King* by T. H. White including

- o *The Sword in the Stone* (1938)
- o *The Queen of Air and Darkness* (or *The Witch in the Wood*) (1939)
- o *The Ill-Made Knight* (1940)
- o *The Candle in the Wind* (1958)
- o *The Book of Merlyn* (1958)

*King Arthur and His Knights of the Round Table* (1953) by Roger Lancelyn Green

*The Acts of King Arthur and His Noble Knights* (1975) by John Steinbeck

# EDITOR'S NOTES

In the 1990's I was a very avid collector of illustrated books, especially those from the "Golden Age" illustrators - Arthur Rackham, Edmund Dulac, Kay Nielsen and NC Wyeth. While collecting Dulac's I was fortunate to meet Ann Hughey while she was just finishing her bibliography of Dulac's works. I had collected a good example of most of Dulac's published works, but the paintings for *The American Weekly* from 1924-1951 remained elusive. Some of the early series were reprinted in other British magazines, but the entire collection had never been reproduced after the initial publication in *The American Weekly* Sunday Supplement.

After a few years of searching libraries and magazine collections I found a complete collection of all *The American Weekly's* at The Academy of Comic Art in San Francisco. The curator, Bill Blackbeard, allowed us to remove all 106 Dulac's and have them professionally photographed. I guarded the transparencies until 2021 when I had them digitally scanned into high quality files.

We published *The American Weekly Covers of Edmund Dulac* the first book of the complete collection in 2021. This is the second book to come from the collection. Our next will be *8 Canterbury Tales* from 1942 which also has text written by John Erskine.

During more than 50 years of publication *The American Weekly* magazine featured some of the most famous and talented illustrators of the era. We hope to be able to locate and photograph more of these wonderful series for future publications.

**Albert Seligman**
Editor

www.ingramcontent.com/pod-product-compliance
Lightning Source LLC
Chambersburg PA
CBHW041606240626
47164CB00008B/188